BOC

Writte
Translat

CW01645530

The Leopard

BY GIUSEPPE TOMASI DI LAMPEDUSA

BrightSummaries.com

GIUSEPPE TOMASI DI LAMPEDUSA

ITALIAN NOVELIST AND SHORT STORY WRITER

- **Born in Palermo in 1896**
- **Died in Rome in 1957**
- **Notable works:**
    - *The Leopard* (1958), novel
    - *The Professor and the Siren* (1961), collection of short stories

A member of the Sicilian aristocracy, Giuseppe Maria Fabrizio Salvatore Stefano Vittorio Tomasi, Duke of Palma and Prince of Lampedusa (1896-1957), is the author of just one novel and several literary studies, notably on Stendhal. He died just after writing *The Leopard*. His career was primarily a military one, and Tomasi went to both world wars as a lieutenant. In 1932 he married Alessandra Wolff-Stormersee, a psychoanalyst who had grown up in St Petersburg. Like the hero of his novel, Tomasi died in a hotel in Palermo before his book was published.

THE LEOPARD

SICILY, PASSION AND MELANCHOLY

- **Genre:** historical novel
- **Reference edition:** Tomasi di Lampedusa, G. (1960) *The Leopard*. Trans. Colquhoun, A. United Kingdom: Collins; Harvill P.
- **First edition:** 1958
- **Themes:** Italian history, aristocracy, decline, death, solitude, ambition

The Leopard tells the story of the fall of a royal family and, through this, the fate of all the Sicilian aristocracy at the time of Italian unification. The novel mixes different genres: mainly historical, it also has an autobiographical dimension and is characterised by the importance given to the hero's subjectivity.

Upon its publication in 1958, despite winning the *Premio Strega* (Italian equivalent of the Booker Prize), *The Leopard* was not immediately well received by the public. Neorealism, which generally uses unembellished descriptions of contemporary society and praises antifascism, was then dominating the Italian literary and film scene.

The Leopard is now considered an Italian literary classic and is compulsory teaching in Italian schools. The very faithful film adaptation directed by Visconti won the *Palme d'Or* at Cannes in 1963.

SUMMARY

THE START OF A NEW ERA

The novel opens on a recital of the rosary, and the description of the Prince of Salina, Don Fabrizio, his palace in Palermo, the Kingdom of the Two Sicilies, and his family. The Prince of Salina is part of the former Italian aristocracy, whom he represents in the text. He is an educated and powerful man.

In May 1860, Don Fabrizio, the prince, has a political conversation with his nephew, Tancredi, whom he loves more than he loves his own children. Later on, he learns that his daughter, Concetta, is in love with Tancredi, and disapproves of this relationship, which he believes is unworthy of the latter. Tancredi is an ambitious character, ready to do anything to achieve his aims.

At the time, Italy is undergoing many changes and is entering the period known as the *Risorgimento*, which will lead to the country's unification and the creation of a national sentiment. "If we want things to stay as they are, things will have to change" (p. 10), explains the prince to his nephew. Tancredi wants to join the supporters of Victor Emmanuel II, who are in favour of Italian unification. Don Fabrizio, like the rest of the Sicilian aristocracy, is afraid of seeing his privileges abolished by this unification, which would imply the amalgamation of the Kingdom of the Two Sicilies to the rest of Italy and the fall of King Francis II, who then reigned in Palermo. Unfortunately for him, the following day, he learns that General Garibaldi has arrived in Marsala to fight for the creation of the Italian state.

Don Fabrizio then goes to the observatory of Father Pirrone, his friend and confidant. They both discuss the recent political events and the changes to come: the arrival of the middle class as the new dominant class and the fate of the Church. The two men then take to their shared passion, studying the movement of the stars.

During their holidays, the prince and his family go to their land in Donnafugata: "he loved the house at Donnafugata, the people, the sense of feudal ownership surviving there" (p. 17). But Don Fabrizio finds that his town has changed, particularly with the rise to fortune of Don Calogero Sedara, head of the liberals, who has become as rich as he is. He sees "revolution in that white tie and two black tails" (p. 23) that Sedara is wearing. Moreover, their personalities differ. These differences are explained through the metaphors of the leopard and the jackal. However, as time passes and the prince starts to get to know Sedara, the social differences that he saw at the beginning between the two of them start to fade. The prince also recognises Sedara's pragmatic intelligence. Angelica, his daughter, immediately charms Tancredi with her great beauty and wealth. At the same time, we learn about his possible relationship with a common girl, symbolised by forbidden fruit.

A short while later, Tancredi asks the prince's permission to marry Angelica. Stella, Don Fabrizio's wife, reacts with indignation, while he seems in favour of the marriage, which is nonetheless unsuitable. Others, such as Don Ciccio, equally disapprove of this union: "How foul, Excellency! [...] It's the end of the Falconeris, and of the Salinas too" (p. 35).

When Father Pirrone goes to see his family in San Cono – which allows the author to describe the conditions of peasant life – he has to sort out a complex family situation. Angelina, his niece, who is three months pregnant, was seduced by Turi's son, who is from an enemy branch of the family. The feud goes back two generations and started with the theft of some almond trees. The same thing seems to be true of the marriage between Angelica and Tancredi: the same sensuality and lure of money are behind it.

While they are out hunting, the prince discusses the rigged vote in Donnafugata with Don Ciccio. The subject of the vote was unification. Under pressure from noteworthy local figures, something that is clearly denounced in *The Leopard* ("the stupid annulment of the first expression of liberty ever offered them", p. 33), the Sicilians vote massively in favour of unification: 432 000 in favour and 600 opposed. Paradoxically, the prince votes in favour of unification.

In November 1860, the prince is visited by Chevalley di Monterzuolo. They discuss the differences between the North and South of Italy. Chevalley offers the prince the position as senator of the Kingdom. He refuses due to loyalty to the Bourbons: "We were the Leopards, the Lions; those who'll take our place will be little jackals, hyenas; and the whole lot of us, Leopards, jackals, and sheep, we'll all go on thinking ourselves the salt of the earth" (p. 53).

Two years later, the Salinas and Sedaras go to a ball at the Palazzo Ponteleone. This is Angelica's first experience of this world. Her father is excited by the luxury of the palace, "insensible to its charm, intent on its monetary value" (p. 64). The prince, on the other hand, is tired and hides in the library where he contemplates Greuze's painting, *La Mort du Juste*, and imagines his own demise. But a dance with Angelica reassures him: "at every twirl a year fell from his shoulders" (p. 66). On the way home, they contemplate the stars: "they were distant, they were omnipotent, and at the same time they were docile to his calculation; just the contrary to human beings, always too near, so weak and yet so quarrelsome" (p. 68).

THE END OF AN ERA

Some time later, we find the prince on his deathbed in a shabby hotel in Palermo. He is visited for the last time by Tancredi and his grandson, Fabrizietto. Don Fabrizio reflects bitterly on his life and his family: "the last of the Salinas was really he himself, this gaunt giant now dying on a hotel balcony" (p. 71). Then death arrives, personified in a woman in travellers' clothes.

In May 1910, we discover that the prince's three daughters, including Concetta, have remained unmarried. They are visited at their palace in Palermo by the archdeacon who is inspecting the private oratories of his archdiocese according to the Pope's stipulation: he has to verify the authenticity of the religious relics in the collection the three women have. Their piety, their link to the Nobles of the Robe, which the large number of relics in their collection ought to signify, represents the last symbol of their part in a fallen aristocracy.

Following his inspections, the cardinal of Palermo states that only five of the family's 74 relics are authentic.

Concetta, in her bedroom which hosts an "inferno of mummified memories" (p. 75), contemplates her now useless trousseau. She is visited by Angelica, whose life is threatened by illness, then by Senator Tassoni. Concetta seems to be an authentic Salina, however much her father underestimated her. At the end of the novel, she gets rid of Bendico, the prince's dog, who is already dead and stuffed, and whose worn out fur resembles that of a leopard.

CHARACTER STUDY

DON FABRIZIO, PRINCE OF SALINA

The main character of the novel, Don Fabrizio is a descendent of former Sicilian aristocracy on his father's side, but of German origin on his mother's side. Described as a powerful, tall and impulsive man, the prince seems to resemble Zeus or Poseidon. His physical appearance also gives him an air of a lion, which thus links him to a leopard, the main feature of the Salina family's coat of arms. He has seven children by his wife, Maria Stella, but seems to prefer Tancredi Falconieri, his nephew.

The prince can be distinguished especially by his ambivalence and the complexity of his character. The charming man engages in astronomy as a scientist, and the internal focus of the novel reveals the richness of his inner life and his intellectual aspirations. The subjectivity of the prince is emphasised in the work, who is proud, brazen, melancholy, sensual, contemplative, angry and kindly all at once.

Finally the prince, through his character, fate and choices, seems to symbolise the entire aristocracy. The Risorgimento, the Italian revolution which leads to reunification, rightly worries this ageing man who wonders about the consequences of political and social change on the aristocracy and the former feudal system.

TANCREDI FALCONIERI

The prince's young nephew, his favourite, is charming, mocking, matches the stereotype of the ambitious social climber and has a great understanding of political events. His decision to marry Angelica, although it initially seems to fit a romantic ideal, in fact stems from a financial calculation.

Tancredi's fate seems to be the opposite of that of the prince. Don Fabrizio's decline corresponds to the irresistible social ascension and youth of Tancredi. But Tancredi's dishonourable behaviour prevents him from being considered as the last representative of the Salina family, the leopards.

FATHER PIRRONE

Father Pirrone is the clergy member of the Salina house. He is inseparable from the Prince of Salina, with whom he forms a pleasant-looking duo. He is a Jesuit and a gifted mathematician, and acquires a complexity throughout the novel that perhaps even makes him the most important character after the prince. The fifth section, which is entirely dedicated to him, allows us to learn more about this character who, until then, has been overshadowed by the splendour of Don Fabrizio: his humble origin and the great respect he commands are mentioned for the first time. Father Pirrone demonstrates a great dexterity and a certain knowledge of human nature during the family feuds.

Father Pirrone is dealt with subtly: the narrator views him in a gently mocking fashion, and he will no longer have a place in the new society as it is based on the death of the Leopard. Additionally, religion, represented in the final chapter by the clergy, no longer has the pleasant and good-natured tolerance of human weaknesses that Father Pirrone has.

DON CALOGERO SEDARA

Sedara is Angelica's father. While Don Fabrizio is a leopard and Tancredi is a falcon, Sedara is described in the novel as a jackal. A representative of the corrupt middle class, triumphant at the time of Italian unification, Sedara is the subject of many satirical remarks by the narrator: vulgar, materialistic and ridiculous, only his practical intelligence, cunning and business sense end up rousing the prince's interest.

Sedara is the exact opposite of the prince and represents the new man, the new middle class that has just taken over power from the failing aristocracy.

FEMALE CHARACTERS

Female characters, daughters of Eve or Mary, are not portrayed favourably in the novel. This depiction is, in a way, faithful to the status of women in Sicily which, in the 19th century, was chauvinistic to say the least.

The women of the Salina family in particular are often described as pious and submissive. They are resistant to change and their attitude verges on ridiculous. Raised according to the customs of the time, they are all devoted, unaware of political matters and firmly attached to the superficial symbols of their belonging to the aristocracy.

In this portrait of the Salina family, Concetta, one of the prince's daughters, is a notable exception: of all the prince's children, she is the only one to benefit from certain passages of inner thoughts. She seems to be a true Salina, although a victim sacrificed at the altar to history and pragmatism. Rejected by Tancredi, whom she is in love with, she also takes on the dimension of a tragic heroine in the novel.

Angelica is differentiated in a splendid way from the other women in the novel. She is extremely beautiful and embodies movement and sensuality. But the narrator also reveals her profoundly hypocritical, ambitious and superficial nature to us. She is portrayed as a corrupting daughter of Eve, who manages, despite her unknown origins, to marry an aristocrat. The viper or she-wolf of the novel, she is also the embodiment of male fantasies and Tancredi's double.

ANALYSIS

AN HISTORICAL NOVEL

The Leopard is an historical novel, meaning that it mixes real events with fictional elements. On the one hand, *The Leopard* gives an accurate account of the historical events that marked 19th-century Italy and is the product of real research work. On the other hand, it presents fictional characters, notably the Salina family, who never existed, but who seem to be inspired by Tomasi's ancestors themselves. In line with the historical novel genre, all the fictional events and characters are realistic in the context of historical truth.

Factual history is the novel's backdrop. The fate of the Prince of Salina has the Risorgimento as its backdrop and central issue, the major episode of Italian history which led to the unification of the country as we know it today. *The Leopard*, in fact, begins at the moment Garibaldi, the Italian general, political leader and key player in the Risorgimento, arrives in Marsala, Sicily, on 11 May 1860. At the time, Italy is divided into three parts, the Papal states, the North under the authority of King Victor Emmanuel II who is supported by the Austrians, and the South, known as the Kingdom of the Two Sicilies, where Francis II reigns. Garibaldi's victorious expedition subjects Sicily's aristocracy and king to Victor Emmanuel II. In Chapter 3 of *The Leopard*, we are presented with the organisation and the results of the vote arranged by Victor Emmanuel II on 21 October 1861, in which the Sicilians must vote on unification. The importance of the dates at the beginning of each section, the reminder of the main events of a problematic era, the mention of people who really existed (such as Garibaldi), as well as the realistic description of life at the time all contribute to making this work a historical novel.

It is, however, the central character's point of view, a member of the aristocracy, that dominates the text: the Risorgimento, the unification of the Two Sicilies to the Kingdom of Italy and social upsets are viewed through the eyes of a witness who maintains some distance from the events. Thus, it is above all the upset of social relationships between the middle class and the aristocracy that are the plot's main axis. Finally, the events are suggested rather than explicitly described. They are, above all, the subject of memories, conversations and are most generally presented in free indirect speech.

The novel hinges on the interplay of social forces, embodied by various characters in the novel:

- Don Fabrizio represents the worn-out aristocracy, trapped by their own traditions. Throughout the novel, however, the prince begins to demonstrate a certain lucidity and thus takes on, for example, the unavoidable thought of the end of the world as he knew it.
- Don Calogero, who has suddenly risen to fortune, evidently represents the rising middle class. Intelligent and unscrupulous, he is a character in search of power.
- Tancredi is a false hero in a way, who is well adapted to this ambiguous revolution.

Tomasi's work maintains a distinct pessimism towards the

events described. No social group escapes Tomasi's disillusioned and ironic view, as he seems to generally criticise the lack of ideals and values and the relentlessness of the time that is passing. It seems, above all, following Tomasi's line of thought, that while hope can no longer be sought in nobility, the recent events also give reason for pessimism as to the future of politics. The vote held is a "maiming of souls" (p. 32); the grotesque mythification of Garibaldi and the missed opportunity for democracy are harshly criticised. The new powers do nothing more than the old ones, and the same archaism increases the gap between the North and the South, with Sicily remaining unchanged and poor.

A METAPHYSICAL REFLECTION ON MAN AND HIS RELATIONSHIP TO TIME AND DEATH

The Leopard is a novel about decline: its main character contemplates the crumbling of the world, powerless to do anything. The economic and spiritual decline of the aristocracy is shown through the description of their flawed ostentation, the abandoned palaces and the infertility of the three unmarried sisters. But it is also, as Don Fabrizio's character suggests, the end of a way of living and a certain way of thinking.

Death is omnipresent. The prince has "courted death", in the words of Tancredi, and often seems affected by a sombre melancholy. Death appears elsewhere, personified in the figure of Venus by Don Fabrizio and, before *La Mort du juste* by Greuze, the prince anticipates his own death. The representation of death is portrayed exceptionally in the seventh chapter of *The Leopard*: the experience of it is given from the point of view of a dying man and this therefore allows the reader to identify with it. This perspective on death is only rarely adopted in literature (Proust, *Les Plaisirs et les Jours* and Tolstoy, *The Death of Ivan Ilyich*). Finally, we must note the many realistic depictions of death that feature throughout the text, for example the dead soldier found in the garden in Chapter 1, or the rotting animal carcasses.

The novel is a questioning of the respective positions of change and eternity: faced with changes in history, the prince desires eternity, which can be seen most notably through his works on astronomy. Equally, his love for Sicily, with its unchanging landscapes, relates to his desire for eternity: "the incessant winds harping their own sorrows on the parched surfaces, today, yesterday, tomorrow, forever and forever" (p. 64). The prince is in search of eternity, maybe of a certain transcendence that will, despite the hazards of political life, bring him calm, comfort and joy.

A SUBJECTIVE WRITING STYLE

It is an omniscient narrator, external to the story, who takes charge of the text. However, we cannot deny that the dominant point of view is that of the Prince of Salina. The prince's thoughts are often revealed to us through the frequent use of interior monologue, which is only rarely used for the other characters (apart from the chapter dedicated to Father Pirrone, which allows us to see the events from another point of view). There is frequently, however, ambiguity as to the origin of the opinions given: are they the narrator's or Don Fabrizio's?

Thanks to the use of interior monologue, the reader enters the prince's mind: we see the thoughts of a rational and thoughtful man, and the countless nuances of his personality: we discover his loneliness, his doubts, his pessimism, his view of Sicily and so forth, which illustrate a true philosophy of existence. The lack of interior monologue for the other characters generally strengthens our impression of the prince's loneliness and the incoherent nature of the failing aristocracy.

Interior monologue also allows the reader to identify and empathise with the prince as we experience his complexity and solitude. It generally gives the work a powerful, moving tone. Finally, it allows the reader to benefit from Don Fabrizio's knowledge, to enter the 'other world' of the aristocracy and to understand its rules and unique refinements. It is also through the prince's reflections that we learn what has happened in the time that has passed between each chapter.

FURTHER REFLECTION

SOME QUESTIONS TO THINK ABOUT...

- What links does Tomasi Di Lampedusa establish between humans and animals in *The Leopard*?
- What place is given to religion in the novel?
- What vision of love emerges from Tomasi's novel?
- Why, in your opinion, does the novel not end at the end of Chapter 7, with the prince's death?
- What makes *The Leopard* a historical novel?
- Why, in your opinion, did Tomasi decide to portray Don Fabrizio as a scientist, particularly as an astronomer?
- Can we consider the fifth chapter of the novel, dedicated to Father Pirrone, as a digression?

We want to hear from you!
Leave a comment on your online library
and share your favourite books on social media!

FURTHER READING

REFERENCE EDITION

- Tomasi di Lampedusa, G. (1960) *The Leopard*. Trans. Colquhoun, A. United Kingdom: Collins; Harvill P.

REFERENCE STUDIES

- Crippa, S. (2007) *Le Guépard*. Paris: Hatier.

ADAPTATIONS

- *The Leopard* (1963) [Film]. Luchino Visconti. Dir. Rome: Titanus.
  This film adaptation of Tomasi's book is extremely faithful to the novel, and won the *Palme d'Or* at Cannes in 1963. It is particularly remarkable for the accuracy of its reconstruction of Sicily. Visconti, whose early works were at the origin of the neorealism trend, was accused of demonstrating a dated classicism with *The Leopard*. Visconti's film, however, beyond its ideological questions, helped to illustrate the novel's universal value, by highlighting the anguished existential search of its main character.

www.brightsummaries.com

Ebook EAN: 9782806280947

Paperback EAN: 9782806287694

Legal Deposit: D/2016/12603/659

Digital conception by Primento, the digital partner of publishers.

19500941R00015

Printed in Great Britain
by Amazon